# RETURN OF THE
# WEREWOLF

## BULLSEYE CHILLERS

# RETURN OF THE

# WEREWOLF

By Les Martin

Illustrated by Karen Chandler

**BULLSEYE CHILLERS™**

**RANDOM HOUSE** 🏠 **NEW YORK**

A BULLSEYE BOOK PUBLISHED BY RANDOM HOUSE, INC.

*Library of Congress Cataloging-in-Publication Data:*
Martin, Les.
Return of the werewolf / by Les Martin.
    p.   cm. — (Bullseye chillers)
SUMMARY: Smitten with a beautiful countess, Sherlock Holmes's cousin
agrees to unmask the killer who's been savaging her ancestral village.
ISBN 0-679-84189-X (pbk.)
[1. Horror stories.]   I. Title.   II. Series.
PZ7.M36353Re   1993   92-47289

Manufactured in the United States of America   10 9 8 7 6 5 4 3 2 1

# Chapter 1

My name is Jonathan Holmes. Unless you are a scholar, you probably never have heard of me. I teach history at Oxford University in England. I also write books on ancient folklore. Few students attend my classes. Even fewer people read my books.

I am sure, though, that you have heard of my cousin. He is Sherlock Holmes, the famous detective.

Sherlock is one of those few people who read my books. He even has sent me letters praising them.

That is why he asked me to pay him a visit. It was a September evening in the year l903.

His message was urgent. It came by telegraph. I wired him back that I would come at once.

I took the train from Oxford to London. At Paddington Station, I hailed a cab. I told the driver to take me to 22lB Baker Street. Through the cab window, I saw the yellow blur of gaslit streetlamps in swirling fog. I heard the *clippety-clop* of the cab horse's hooves on the cobblestoned street.

"A foul night out," I told Sherlock when he opened his door. Like most Englishmen, I feel most comfortable talking about the weather.

Sherlock, however, had no interest in small talk. "Good to see you," he said. "I badly need your help. Come warm yourself by the fire. Let me introduce you to my guest. And to a most fascinating mystery."

A well-dressed young woman was sitting before the fireplace. I judged her to be in her early twenties. I also judged her to be the most beautiful woman I had ever seen.

Her hair was blond. Her eyes were blue. Her skin was fair. And her features were perfect.

"Allow me to introduce the Countess Marie de La Coste," Sherlock said. "Countess, this is my cousin Jonathan Holmes. Let me assure you, he is as brilliant in his field as I am in mine."

"Then you must be very brilliant, indeed," she said. She spoke excel-

lent English with a charming French accent.

We shook hands. Our eyes met.

Do you believe in love at first sight? I never had—until that evening.

For an endless moment, I gazed into her blue eyes. She did not turn those eyes away.

Sherlock's voice broke the spell. "Let us waste no time. There is none to waste. Please, Countess, tell Jonathan the story you told me."

I sat down in an armchair facing her. I looked into her eyes again. But now she was no longer looking into mine. Fear filled her eyes. As I listened to her story, I saw why.

## Chapter 2

The Countess Marie de La Coste came from the Ardeche region in the southern part of France. Her family had lived in the same chateau there for six hundred years. Her mother had died giving birth to her. Her father died when she was only one. Fortunately, her brother, Phillipe, was fifteen years older than she was. He became both father and mother to her.

Then, six months ago, her brother died in a hunting accident. At this point, Marie broke off her story.

"Tell me, do you believe in werewolves?" she asked.

"Once I would have said no without question," I said. "But last year I wrote a book about the werewolf legend. The number of stories I found surprised me. I found tales about werewolves from around the world.

"They did not completely change my mind," I continued. "Men who turn into killer wolves under a full moon still seem hard to believe. But there are too many accounts to easily deny. I have yet to find a reasonable explanation for them."

"Where I come from, we take werewolves seriously," Marie said. "Stories about them have been passed down from parent to child for centuries. My brother had a strange sense of duty. He protected not only our chateau but the local village from werewolves. Now I know how right he was. The horror began after his death."

Spellbound, I listened to Marie tell of that horror.

"The first full moon after Phillipe

died, the werewolf struck. Emile the baker was found ripped apart in the forest," she said. "The next full moon, his widow Sabine and her two small children were found half eaten in their field. Since then even more have died. The beast has gotten bolder and bolder. And perhaps hungrier and hungrier."

Marie paused to calm her trembling voice. Then she went on. "That is why I came to England to see Mr. Sherlock Holmes. I read how he solved the case of the Hound of the Baskervilles. I thought he might be interested in an even more terrifying case."

"I would have been happy to take the case," Sherlock said. He took his pipe from his mouth. "But I am busy with an affair of the greatest importance. I can only say it involves the royal family and the peace of Europe. Fortunately, though, I thought of you, Jonathan. You are the perfect person to aid the Countess."

"Why me?" I asked.

Sherlock smiled and said, "First, as you said, you are an expert on the werewolf legend. Second, your mind is keen. And, third, I consider it a crime that you live so much in the world of books. It is time you entered the real world."

I might have argued with Sherlock. But I could not argue with Marie.

"Please, say you will help me," she begged. "The next full moon is only ten days away."

"Well," I said. "Classes do not begin for several weeks. And I was thinking of getting away for a brief holiday."

"Then you will!" Marie exclaimed.

"Splendid," Sherlock said.

"I even will come well prepared," I said. I smiled to myself. "As you know, Sherlock, I am a keen fencer."

"And a good thing, too," Sherlock said. "It's managed to keep a book-worm like you in decent shape."

"Last year I won my fencing club championship," I went on. "As a prize, my fellow members gave me *this*."

I held up the finely carved walking stick I carried. Smoothly I drew out the sword concealed in it.

"It's a bit of a joke," I said. "My friends had the blade made of sil-ver—in honor of my book on were-wolves."

Sherlock chuckled. "Quite good. Only something silver can kill one of these creatures, I believe."

"So the legend goes," I said.

But Marie was not smiling. "I only pray you will not need it," she said.

# Chapter 3

Marie had come to England with her maid, a middle-aged woman named Denise. Denise acted as chaperone on our trip to France. Marie and I were able to travel together without causing scandal.

The journey was not easy. First we had to go to Paris by boat and train. From Paris, we took a train south to the city of Avignon. Marie's coach met us there. It was an old coach, with an old driver. But the horses were young. We made good time on the road west to the Ardeche.

The landscape changed. The hills

rose higher. The valleys plunged deeper. The forests grew thicker. There were fewer farms and vineyards. There were more herds of goats and sheep. They grazed in fields where grass was broken by jutting rock. The Ardeche was beautiful. But its beauty was wild and harsh.

By now, Marie and I had come to know each other better. The more we knew, the stronger the bond between us grew.

"It is amazing how alike we are," Marie said at one point.

I agreed. It *was* amazing. She was a twenty-year-old French noblewoman. I was a thirty-year-old English scholar. Yet we shared so much.

Both of us had led such sheltered lives. Marie had never before left her native region. Her brother had brought teachers to the chateau for her. She learned her English from them and from the books in the chateau's library. She learned everything else she knew of the outside world the same way.

I was not much more at home in the outside world. My life had been spent in schools and libraries. I learned my French from teachers and books. It was the same way she learned her English.

Even in smaller ways, we were so very alike. We admired the same authors, the same artists, the same composers. We found the same things moving and the same things funny. We even discovered we were both vegetarians.

"Ever since I was a little girl," Marie said, "I have found the idea of eating flesh disgusting. I don't see how anyone does it."

"I did eat meat—until I was twenty," I confessed. "But reading and thinking changed my mind. I share your view completely now."

We were sitting in a swaying railway dining car. We looked at each other over our plates of potatoes, broccoli, and salad.

I did not dare say what else I hoped we shared.

I barely dared to even hope it.

It seemed impossible that she might return the feeling I had for her. Yet by the time we reached the chateau, I had begun to think it just might be possible.

But now was not the time to find out. Now was not the time to talk of love. Not when we stood looking out the window at the night sky. The white moon shone bright. In a week it would be full.

Marie stared at it bleakly.

"Soon I will start having the terrible dreams again," she said.

"The dreams?" I said. "You have never spoken of dreams."

"I am ashamed of them," Marie said. "They make me sound like a frightened little schoolgirl. They

come from hearing werewolf stories since I was a child. That's what my brother said. I'm sure he was right."

"What kind of dreams?" I asked. Without thinking, I put my hand on her shoulder. I felt her trembling.

"Dreams of horror," she said. "Dreams of faces screaming. Dreams of flesh torn open. Dreams of blood gushing. As the full moon approaches, I start having them."

She turned toward me. "Please, you must help me," she said. "You must help all who live here. Please, end the nightmare."

The chill of her fear went through me like a shiver. I made an effort to keep my voice strong and steady.

"I will," I promised. But I had to add, "I will—if I can."

# Chapter 4

"It is the villagers who have the most to fear," Marie told me.

It was the next day. We were walking to the village, two miles away. The road was hard-packed dirt and stone. It cut through a thick forest of pines and chestnut trees. The sun flashed through the branches. The moon of the night before was gone—but not forgotten.

"I myself am safe," Marie said. "My brother saw to that. He believed in the werewolf. He vowed it would never get me. An ironworker put bars on my bedroom window.

And bolts on the door.

"My brother made sure my door was bolted every full moon," she continued. "He even made our servants leave the chateau that night—in case one of them had the curse."

"He must have loved you very much," I said.

"He did," Marie said. "After his death, I found out how much. Our lawyer gave me a letter from my brother. He wrote it in case he died before I did. Phillipe begged me to continue keeping myself safe above all. And I have."

"See that you keep it up," I said. "I don't want to have to worry about you when the full moon comes. And I would—very much."

Marie smiled shyly but tenderly.

"Thank you for caring," she said. "But it is the villagers you must think about. They are the ones who have been killed every full moon since my brother passed away."

She paused. "They look to me for help. My family ruled here for many centuries. The villagers still turn to the chateau in times of trouble."

We had reached an old stone bridge. It crossed a streambed. There was only a trickle of water. After the autumn rains it would be a torrent.

The village was on the other side of the bridge. Its rough stone buildings had slanting slate roofs. None of the buildings were more than three stories high. There was no telling how old they were. Whether built five years ago or five hundred, all were built the same way. It was a village where time had stopped.

I was not surprised to see five-pointed stars painted on buildings. Those stars were called pentagrams. They were supposed to guard against werewolves. People held on to old beliefs in this ancient village.

As we walked through the narrow, winding cobblestoned streets, I saw that some pentagrams were faded with age. But others were fresh.

I mentioned this to Marie.

"For almost twenty years before my brother's death, the werewolf did not strike," Marie said. "People started to think the curse was gone. They stopped painting the pentagrams. But now, as you see—"

She turned toward an old man. At that very moment he was painting a pentagram on a wall. He stopped working to tip his cloth cap.

"Good work, Charles," she said. "I am glad you are doing what I suggested."

"It was kind of you to care about me, my lady," the old man said. "I have gotten so lazy as I grow old." He gave a cracked chuckle. "I thought that maybe the monster would not be interested in dried-up meat like me."

"Don't talk like that," Marie said to him. "I expect to celebrate your birthday ten years from now."

"Yes, my lady. Thank you, my lady," the old man answered. He tipped his cap again as we went on.

"I try to keep up my family's tradition," Marie told me. "I want to take care of the villagers as if they were my own children. But I feel so helpless against that hideous werewolf."

"I'm sure the villagers are grateful

to you," I said. "I could see it in that old man's eyes."

But when we reached the town square, I saw a far different look in a villager's eyes. We had stopped at a small outdoor cafe. As the waiter wiped the marble tabletop, the look he gave the Countess was very close to hate.

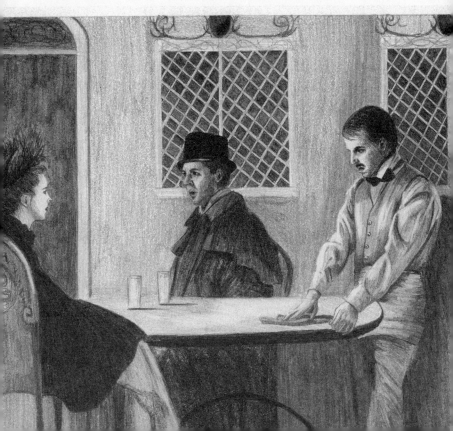

Fortunately, Marie was looking the other way. She did not notice it. But I kept remembering that strange look. I could not get it out of my mind. Even as I was being introduced to the town priest. Even as I shook hands with the town policeman. That strange look stayed with me.

I was like a bloodhound that had picked up a promising scent.

The next day I returned alone to the café to follow it.

# Chapter 5

The waiter in the café was also the owner. To win him over, I ordered his most expensive champagne. I invited him to share the bottle of sparkling wine with me.

The champagne was very good. I nursed my glass to keep my head clear. But he drank greedily. By the third glass, his tongue was loose.

"You are a good sort, Englishman," he said. "So I will give you good advice. Leave the chateau. And forget about the Countess. I know you find her beautiful. But the chateau is an evil place. And the Countess comes from an evil family."

"The Countess—evil?" I said. How could I believe such a thing!

"Oh, not her," the waiter said. "But the men of the family are different. The foolish people in this village think the counts de La Coste have protected them. But my father told me a story that his father had told him. A story as old as the curse that has shadowed the village for as long as men remember."

"And that story?" I asked.

"Perhaps I should not tell you," he said. "You will not believe it. You are too dazzled by the Countess."

"Not at all," I said. "I can see you are an honest man. And a man who knows what's what. But have some more wine. Talking makes your throat dry."

I filled his glass. He took a long

swallow. Then he wiped his mustache with the back of his hand.

"My father told me the counts did not protect us. They preyed on us," he said. "The curse of the werewolf was in their blood. Each of them reached a certain age. Then he became that hellish beast."

"That makes no sense," I protested. "The last Count de La Coste is dead. Only with his death did the attacks begin. The Countess told me herself. Do you say she was lying?"

"I say she does not know the truth," the waiter said. He paused. I refilled his glass. He drank and ran his tongue over his thick lips. "I say you should ask her if she *saw* her brother dead. I say she only saw a sealed coffin. I say her brother still lives—and kills."

"And I say you talk nonsense," said

a voice from the next table. The man wore a black suit. He had rimless glasses. His beard was neatly trimmed.

"Let me introduce myself," he said. "I am Alphonse Daudet. I apologize for butting in. But I can see you are an educated man like myself. Please don't think that we French are all superstitious peasants. We don't all believe wild tales."

"No," said the waiter with a growl. "Some of us are idiotic schoolteachers come here from Paris."

Alphonse Daudet sighed. "You see what a man of culture and science has to put up with around here. I will be happy when the school year is over and I can find another job. It will be like returning from the Middle Ages to the twentieth century."

"I take it you don't believe in werewolves," I said.

"Of course not," he said with contempt. "Do you?"

"I try to keep my mind open," I said. "I am doing research on the subject. I came here to investigate rumors. The Countess was kind enough to offer me lodging."

"You will find that the story of the werewolf is a fairy tale," Daudet assured me. "If they had a modern police force here, the killer would have been caught. Clearly a madman is loose."

"The only one who is mad is you," the waiter cut in.

He grabbed the bottle and poured the last of the champagne. He drank it in an angry gulp.

"It is crazy not to admit the truth right before your eyes. I have a question for you, Englishman. Why do you think there are no pentagrams at the chateau? I ask you, why?" repeated the waiter.

"Actually, I did ask the Countess," I said. "She told me that her family was too proud to bow to fear. It is a point of honor. 'Pride above all.' That is the motto on the family coat of arms."

"It is more than pride," said a voice from a table behind me.

I turned to see an old man in simple country clothes. Though his hair was white, his head was held high.

He had strong features, and a defiant gaze.

"It is faith," he said. "Faith in the power of good over evil. Faith in the power of light over darkness. Faith in the power of the Lord over the devil. I too have that faith. I too refuse to put a pentagram on my house. Although my house is only a humble cottage, not a grand chateau."

The waiter smiled sourly.

"Englishman, please meet Charles Dupont," he said. "Dupont believes that goodness can protect him from the werewolf. At least, that is what he says. Others think differently. They say that he does not fear the werewolf because he is—" The waiter stopped there. "I will not say more. I leave the rest to your imagination."

"Do not believe him," the old man said. "He is like all the others here—

men of no faith."

"It is not the power of faith they lack," the schoolteacher argued. "It is the power of scientific knowledge."

As for myself, I still had to find what I so badly lacked.

The truth.

## Chapter 6

I hated to ask Marie the question I had to ask her. But I had to pursue the truth.

We sat over coffee at the dinner table. Marie's face was angelic by candlelight. It should have been a time of perfect happiness.

But for me a shadow fell over the scene. It was a monstrous shadow of a giant wolf. I could almost see it crouching, ready to spring. I could almost see its teeth, its claws.

Through the window I saw the moon. It was larger than the night before. It seemed to set off a clock

ticking in my brain. There was only one way to silence it.

I started, as gently as I could. "Your brother's death must have come as a terrible shock."

"It was terrible," Marie said, her face clouding.

"A hunting accident, you said?" I went on.

"Yes," Marie said. "His manservant described it. Phillipe must have tripped. His loaded gun went off— right into his face."

"How ghastly," I said. "It must have been a hideous wound."

"I hate to imagine it," she said.

"Then you did not see it?" I asked.

"I was already in shock," Marie said. "They thought the sight would be too much for me. They buried my brother in a sealed coffin."

"Who were 'they'?" I asked.

"The family servants," said Marie. "I could not have gotten through the ordeal without them. They are so loyal. They took care of everything."

"You must miss your brother terribly," I said.

"I do, of course," Marie said. "Yet, in a way, it is almost as if he were not gone."

I leaned forward. "Not gone? What do you mean by that?"

"It's as if I can feel him still protecting me," Marie said. "In a way, he is. You may remember the letter our lawyer gave me. It told me to keep guarding myself each night of the full moon. To send the servants out of the chateau. And to keep my door locked."

"Was that all it said?" I asked.

"That was all it said," Marie assured me.

"Your brother left no other writings?" I asked.

"Not that I know of," Marie said. "There may be something in his desk drawer. But the key is with our lawyer. He says my brother left him orders. The drawer may be opened only when the de La Coste family name dies out."

"And are there others besides yourself to carry on that name?" I asked.

"No," Marie said.

"So if you marry, the name will die out," I said.

"It does not have to," Marie said. "At other times when there were only women left in the family, the men they married took the de La Coste name."

"Rather unusual," I commented.

"For commoners, perhaps," Marie said. "But customs are different for families like mine."

"And do you think that you will marry?" I asked. "Is there a man you love? Or has an alliance been arranged with another noble family? I know that marriages among aristocrats often are not made in heaven."

Marie smiled softly. "You are right.

But I would never marry a man I did not love. And if I did love him, his rank in life would not matter."

Marie looked directly into my eyes. No trace of fear was on her face. I saw only love and joy.

Marie had answered my question. It was like being in a dream. But a nightmarish shadow soon fell over it. The shadow of a werewolf.

How would she look at me if I found that her beloved brother lived on as a monster?

What would she do if she ever had to choose between him and me?

I prayed I would never have to find out.

# Chapter 7

Now our love was out in the open. It seemed to take on a life of its own. It grew more and more solid.

Marie and I made plans. Or, rather, I let her make them. I did not have to press her. It took her only a few days to decide. First, she would take my name when we were wed.

"Being a countess has never brought me joy," she said. "Only with you have I known happiness. I think the time of the de La Costes belongs to the past. I want a future—a future bright with love. I want to go to England with you."

I smiled at her. "Do you really want to be a professor's wife?"

"More than anything," she said. "I will give my property to the villagers. Their taxes and labor built the chateau. They are its rightful owners."

"And what about your servants?" I said.

"I will give what wealth I have to them," she said. "Would you want a wife without title or fortune?"

"All I want is you," I assured her.

I put my arm around her shoulders. We had been walking in the great forest that surrounded the chateau. The first fallen chestnuts of autumn lay on the ground. Beyond the forest, the sun blazed lemon-white in a deep blue September sky. But here it was dim and cool. It was an enchanted moment.

"If only we could leave right now," Marie sighed.

"But there is nothing to stop us," I said.

Marie shook her head. "We cannot leave before we end the curse of the werewolf," she said. "It is a debt that I as a de La Coste owe the village."

A chill ran through me. Marie did not suspect how high that debt might be. If the waiter was right, the de La Costes owed the village for hundreds of years of horror.

Of course, his tale might not be true. Marie's brother might truly be dead, not in hiding.

The werewolf might be a lunatic, as the schoolteacher had said. The very word *lunacy* came from the Latin word for the moon—*luna*.

Or what about the old man? Perhaps the villagers' suspicions about him were right.

After my book came out, my cousin Sherlock had asked me a question. Did I myself believe in werewolves? He, of course, as a man of reason, did not.

Now, after days of investigation here, I knew only one thing. The deaths in the village were real. As real as the fear that filled the very air. As real as the web of suspicion that spread so wide.

As real as the moon that tonight would be full.

## Chapter 8

"It is so early to say good night," Marie said.

Through the window we could see an orange sun in the west. Already its lower rim was vanishing. Soon the moon would take its place in the cloudless sky. The huge yellow harvest moon of autumn. The full moon.

"It's just for tonight," I told her.

"Tonight will be the last time I will have to do this," she said. "Tomorrow we will leave here forever.

"I know you will do your best tonight," she continued. "I pray you will find out the truth about the werewolf. I pray you will end its rule of terror. But whether you succeed or not, I will be free. I can go to England with you. I will have done all I could to pay my family debt."

"You will have paid it in full," I assured her.

I walked with her to her room. She paused at the doorway and flung herself into my arms.

"Please be careful," she whispered. "You are more precious to me than life itself."

Was I more precious to her than her beloved brother? I wondered.

"Of course I will be careful," I said to her. "I assure you, I have no intention of losing my life. Not now that I will be sharing it with you."

She smiled at me. "Oh, you are so English. So cool, so calm."

"One of us has to be," I told her. "But there is no time for talking. The moon is already rising."

She nodded. "Until tomorrow, Jonathan," she said.

"Until tomorrow, my dear," I answered.

She entered her room and shut the heavy oak door. I heard her slide the bolt that locked it.

I would have double-locked it from the outside, as her brother used to do. But that side locked with a key. And I had no idea where it might be. Buried with her brother, perhaps—if indeed he was buried. Or else locked away in his desk.

It did not matter. Marie would be safe. She had promised not to slide back the bolt whatever happened. Or whoever might beg to be let in.

I was free to go out into the night.

I suppose I should have felt at least a touch of fear. But, strange to say, I did not. Instead I felt more alive and alert than I had ever felt before.

Why? Was it the challenge of ridding the village of its curse? Or the

chance to rid Marie of her tormenting burden? Or the hope of unmasking the fiendish man or murderous beast behind the killings?

It was partly those things, of course. But deep in my heart I knew otherwise. I would feel this same way without them.

First and foremost, I am a scholar—a born scholar. A scholar in many ways is like a detective. He follows a trail of clues to solve a mystery. I had read all that was written about werewolves. I knew enough about them to know how little I knew!

There were so many conflicting stories about werewolves. There were so many questions those different stories raised. And now I had a chance to find the answers myself.

I walked on the moonlit road

through the forest toward the town. I knew how my cousin Sherlock felt as he neared the climax of a case. I felt the thrill of the chase.

My every nerve was alive. My every sense was fine-tuned to the slightest sight or sound. I saw the silvery leaves swaying in the gentle breeze. I heard the crickets chirping. They made the silence of the night more clear.

Suddenly I froze. I felt as if an electric charge had shot through me.

A hideous howling split the night air. I raced through the forest toward it. My swordstick was clutched firmly in my hand.

A sentence flashed into my mind. It was one that Sherlock loved to use.

*The game was afoot!*

## Chapter 9

*It* was lit by moonlight flooding into the clearing in the forest. *Its* gray fur shone silver in that ghostly light.

*It* was larger than any wolf could ever be. *It* was a huge, sleek beast with rippling muscles.

Long claws curved out from *its* paws. I could see the great yellow fangs in *its* open jaws. Blood dripped from those jaws as *it* turned to face me.

*Its* growling thundered. *It* poised to spring. But then *it* saw the one thing in the world *it* feared. My silver sword blade glinting in the moon-light.

*It* gave a roar of rage. With a single bound, *it* vanished into the forest.

I ran toward the dark shape that lay on the ground. But even as I did so, my scholar's mind made a note of what I had seen.

The folk stories were right: The werewolf had no tail.

I crouched over the man on the ground. I forced myself to look at him. His black suit was shredded. His throat was ripped open. But I still could see who he was. Even if I couldn't, I would have guessed.

Alphonse Daudet, the school-teacher, never again would doubt that werewolves existed. He should have stayed in Paris. There at least his death would be mourned. Here the people would only mock his

memory. They would laugh at the fool who took a walk by moonlight.

I stood upright. I did not have time to stay. There was nothing I could do for Daudet. And the night of the full moon was still young.

I knew where my next stop would be. The home of Charles Dupont, the old man without a pentagram. I had already found out where his house was. Were his suspicious neighbors right? Was his holy faith an unholy lie?

I would find out if the old man was at home tonight. Or if tonight was his night to roam and ravage.

I returned to the road and ran toward the village. I was panting when I reached the old man's stone cottage. It was on the edge of town.

I saw I had not been fast enough.

The window of the cottage was

shattered. The glass had fallen inside. Someone or something had crashed through it from the outside.

I heard moaning from the darkness within. I used my swordstick to clear away the jagged glass. Some was still in the window frame. I carefully climbed inside and lit a match.

Charles Dupont lay on the bare wooden floor. Blood was turning brown on the floorboards around him.

Bending over him, I lit another match. His throat, like Daudet's, was torn open. But he still breathed—in wheezing gasps of pain.

I pulled out a handkerchief to try to stop the flow of blood.

The old man saw me. He made a desperate effort. He shook his white head. He choked out a single word. "No. . ."

It was the last word he would ever say. His breath stopped. The blood no longer bubbled out of his throat.

But it was all he had to say. I realized what he wanted to tell me.

He did not want to live. He knew what happened to anyone who survived a werewolf's attack. It was a fate worse than death.

That person became a werewolf too.

I let my match go out. There was nothing more I could do here. What I had to do was think.

Already the werewolf had claimed two lives. It usually never took more than one in a single night.

Something had increased its hunger. I could make a good guess what that something might be. Anger. Anger at the stranger who had come to hunt it. Anger at me.

Suddenly a thought struck me. The werewolf's rage might go beyond me. It might go to the one who had brought me here.

I thought of the chateau with all the servants gone. A single door stood between Marie and the werewolf.

I could not be sure how much the werewolf knew. But I did know how well Marie's brother must know the chateau. And how well he knew Marie.

If there was anyone who knew the weak spots in both, it was he.

If there was anyone who was the werewolf, it was he.

He might be bounding toward the chateau at this very moment. Even now I might be too late to stop him.

Fear can give a person super-human strength. I still can barely believe how fast I ran. And I was not even out of breath when I entered the chateau and raced to Marie's room.

But my thudding heart seemed to stop when I reached her door.

The door was open.

The werewolf had won.

## Chapter 10

Wild rage filled me. I drew the blade out of my swordstick. I charged through the open door and found—nothing.

The room was empty. Marie was not there. Alive or dead.

Had the werewolf killed her? And had he then carried her away?

I put the blade back in my walking stick. I searched the room for signs of a struggle. But I did not find a trace. Not even, thank God, a spot of blood.

But I did see Marie's nightgown. It lay crumpled on the carpet. I realized what had happened.

Marie must have been worried about me. She had rushed out to look for me. Two people were far

safer than one on the night of the werewolf.

Or perhaps she had another reason for wanting to find me. Perhaps she had remembered something that might help me. Or else had a warning that might save me.

It was even possible that she knew the truth about her brother Phillipe. And she had made her choice. A choice between her loyalty to him and her love for me.

But none of this mattered at the moment. All that mattered was that she was out in the night alone.

Even if the werewolf were her own brother, she would not be spared. I knew enough of werewolves to know that. Not a one had a spark of human feeling.

I had to find her. Protect her. I prayed I could. But as I turned toward the door, my blood ran cold.

I heard it before I saw it. A rumbling growling. Then the huge gray werewolf bounded into the room.

Both of us froze.

The werewolf froze with surprise.

I froze with fear.

Our eyes locked. I found myself looking into eyes of the purest blue.

In spite of my terror, I remembered something. I had read that werewolves kept their human eyes.

My brain was working now. I felt it regaining command of my body.

But the great beast before me still hesitated in its charge. Its flanks were heaving. Its muscles quivering. It looked as if it were fighting against itself. It looked as if it were straining to break free of a leash. An invisible leash that it felt but that I could not see.

Then it did break free.

In a mighty leap, it was upon me.

But its moment of hesitation gave me the time I needed. My blade was out again. I held it in an iron grip as the werewolf lunged. The razor-sharp point entered the pearl-gray chest of the beast.

My blade was up to the hilt in the werewolf's huge body. Then the beast hit me. It smashed me down on my back. I lay helpless under the beast's great weight. I felt the tips of its teeth on my throat. I waited for those mighty jaws to close. And for my life to end.

Instead I felt the crushing weight grow lighter. I felt the hard teeth soften. They were no longer teeth but lips.

I knew without looking that the werewolf was dead.

I knew that when dead the were-wolf returned to its human form.

And I knew what human form now lay on top of me. I felt soft lips against my neck. They were giving a kiss of death.

I turned away my eyes. Gently I withdrew my blade. I kept my eyes turned away. I covered the un-clothed body with a bedsheet.

It was the least I could do. Only if Marie were my wife would I have the right to see her thus.

And now that would never be.

The nightmare of the werewolf was over. My dream of happiness was ended.

All that remained was the mystery of what lay behind the horror.

And I had a very good idea where to find the key to it.

I moved like a mechanical man as

I left the room. All feeling was left behind me—with my dead loved one. Everything I was doing now was an act of memory. I knew my life would be that way for as long as I lived.

All that I had to fall back on was my training. My training as a scholar. A person who seeks the truth.

In the past I looked for truth in libraries. Now I went to the locked desk of Marie's brother. There was no way to pry open the lock. I took an ancient ax from the wall and smashed the fine wood.

I took out the neat pile of papers inside the desk. I lit a gas lamp and sat down. Like a good scholar, I began to read.

# Chapter 11

*I, Phillipe de La Coste, am in sound mind as I write these words. The story I have to tell is not a wild invention. I only wish it were!*

*It pains me to write this. I was raised to be proud of my family. I was raised to defend my family honor. I was raised to put my family above everything else in the world.*

*And now I am betraying my family. I can only defend myself by saying that this will not be read until my family has died out. Or until my beloved sister weds. For, unknown to her, I have given my lawyer an order. He is to give the key to my desk to one man. The man she is to marry. My lawyer will tell him to open it before the wedding day. That is as far as I can go to make sure my family line does die out.*

*But now I will tell the story that I hate to tell. I will begin at the beginning. The beginning for me, at least. For when the real beginning was, I do not know. It is lost in the deep past.*

*For me it began as it will end. Under a full moon. I was fifteen. Like many young men that age, I thought I knew better than my father. He forbade me to go hunting the werewolf that ravaged the region. But I disobeyed. I went out into the forest with rifle in hand. I had loaded the rifle with silver bullets.*

*I had no luck. The moon was low in the sky when I returned to the chateau. I was going to my room when I heard the growling. It came from my sister's nursery.*

My finger was on the rifle trigger as I rushed into the room. I was too late to save my sister's nurse. Her bloody body lay on the floor. But my baby sister still lived. The werewolf's paw was ready to claw her when I fired.

My silver bullet hit the werewolf's heart. It fell lifeless. I did not even give it a glance. I ran to see if my tiny sister was safe. She seemed to be.

But she was not untouched. As the werewolf died, its claw had slashed her little arm.

My sister was crying in pain. But my heart was crying in agony.

Like all who lived in the region, I knew the legend. The legend of the werewolf. I knew that anyone who survived a werewolf's attack would become a werewolf too.

Then I turned to look at the werewolf. For a moment I forgot about my sister.

I was staring at the dead body of my noble father. I had heard the whispered stories about my noble family. Now I knew they were true.

The curse of the werewolf was in our blood!

That night I buried my father. I told the world he had died of a heart attack. No one doubted my word. Who could? I was a de La Coste.

That night I also began to watch over my sister.

Year after year I watched. Every full moon I made sure I alone watched over her.

Year after year I saw nothing to fear. She was a treasure. The light of my life. Her outward beauty was matched by the beauty of her spirit.

Then, at thirteen, she began to change into a woman. It started as my angel of a sister slept. The moon was full.

*I saw the hair sprout from her fair
skin. I saw the jaw forming on her flaw-
less face. I saw her pearly teeth grow
longer and sharper. I saw her delicate
hands and feet turn into paws. I saw her
wake and stare at me. And I heard her*

growl. Then she fell asleep again.

The next day she remembered nothing. She only vaguely recalled having a bad dream. She smiled as she blamed it on the silly local legend. The story of the werewolf.

I knew then what I had to do. I convinced her that the legend was true. I told her that I had not wanted to scare her when she was younger. But that was why I had guarded her every full moon. And now she was old enough to help guard herself.

Every full moon after that, I locked her in her room. I listened to the great beast inside. I heard it bashing against the door. I listened to it howling to get out.

And every morning after, my sister remembered nothing more than a bad dream.

The village stayed safe from the werewolf. And my sister stayed safe from *knowing the horrifying truth about her-self.*

*But now I can no longer make sure of this safety. Not the safety of the village. Not the safety of my dear sister.*

*I have known this would happen ever since I saw my father dead. The only question was when.*

*This year, I turned thirty-five. It start-ed the first full moon after my birthday. I saw the hair growing on my palms. I felt my stomach grow hollow. I had a hunger for something I could not name.*

*Tonight the moon will be full again. But I will not see it rise.*

*My servant will find my dead body to-morrow morning. He will also find a note telling him what to do. He will say I died in a hunting accident. He will make sure I am buried in a sealed coffin. Then he will leave the region. I have left him mon-ey to take care of all his needs.*

*I can only pray that my sister continues to lock herself in her room. I will not be there to double-lock it from the outside.*

*I can only pray that if she weds, her husband will watch over her as I have.*

*I can only pray that they do not have children.*

## Chapter 12

My job here was finished.

As a detective, I had solved the case.

As a scholar, I had added a new chapter to history. To the history of werewolves, that is.

As a man, I had lost the one woman I had ever loved.

There remained only a few loose ends. I had to tie them up before I left.

I returned to Marie's room. I kept my eyes from where she lay on the floor. Instead I looked closely at the bolt inside her door.

Squinting hard, I found what I expected to find. The bolt was covered with scratch marks.

The werewolf had been more than strong, swift, and savage. It had been horribly clever. It had been able to claw open the bolt. When it had returned, it must have clawed the bolt closed. It had been able to cover its tracks.

It must have known what Marie would do if she learned the truth. She would do what her brother had done. She would have killed the werewolf. And there was only one way she could.

But now the werewolf was gone. Now only Marie's body remained. After I had solved that final problem, I would be free to go.

I walked to the village. I took the letter written by Marie's brother with me.

People gathered in groups in the village. Their faces were pale with fear. They talked among themselves in whispers. I knew what they were whispering about. The latest victims of the werewolf had been found.

I went to the house of Charles Dupont. The town policeman was there.

His name was Aristide Briand. Usually, he was a cheerful, kindly man. But now his face was grim. His eyes burned with anger.

"Please, you must read this," I said. I held out the letter.

"Some other time, Englishman," he said with a gruff voice. "Can't you see I am busy?"

"This will tell you who the werewolf was," I said.

He snatched the pages from me. He started to read them eagerly. But as he read, I saw his eagerness fade. His face was filled with a great sadness by the time he finished.

"And the Countess—where is she now?" he asked.

"She is no more," I said. And I told him what had happened.

"At least she is free of the curse," Aristide said.

"Just as the village is," I said.

"I will tell the villagers," Aristide said. "They will no longer have to live in fear."

"And the authorities in Paris. What will you tell them about the murders?" I asked.

Aristide shrugged. "The deaths will remain officially unsolved. We people around here keep our affairs to ourselves. There is no reason to blacken the de La Coste name."

"But there is one person we must tell," I said. "The priest. Marie must have a proper burial."

Aristide nodded. "Let us go to him now. But I can make no promises. It is up to him to decide on the proper thing to do."

The priest, Father Arnaud, listened to our story.

"I am afraid she cannot be buried

on church grounds," he said. "But, fortunately, she does not have to be. The de La Costes have a cemetery of their own, on the chateau grounds. Marie will be buried next to her brother. And I will bless the graves of both of them. May their goodness live for eternity. Now their evil is dead."

"May I attend the ceremony?" I asked.

"Of course, my son," Father Arnaud said.

"And what do you intend to do after that?" Aristide asked me.

There was something in the way he looked at me. Something that was disturbing. But I could not figure out what it was.

"I will return to England," I said.

"You will leave quickly, then?" he persisted.

"By the first train," I said.

"And will you be returning here?" he went on.

"No. Never. It would be too painful," I said. "But why do you ask?"

Silently he showed me the white pages. He pointed to one of them. A drop of blood stained it.

Fresh blood.

My blood.

"You said the werewolf attacked you. Then you killed it," Aristide said.

A chill went through me. I looked down at my hand. I saw a scratch. I had not felt it before that moment. It was the scratch of a claw.

"Yes," I said in a dead voice. "The werewolf attacked me. And I survived."

## Chapter 13

I kept my promise to Aristide. I left the village as soon as Marie was buried. Aristide made it his business to watch me go off.

There are two ways to say "goodbye" in French. *Au revoir* means "until we meet again." *Adieu* is a final farewell. Aristide did not smile as he said, "*Adieu,* Englishman."

I climbed into the carriage. The driver cracked his whip. I smiled bitterly as we sped toward Avignon. I was leaving the village of de La Coste behind. But I was carrying the de La Coste curse with me.

I took the train at Avignon. But I did not go home to England.

In Paris I learned that a ship was leaving for Canada. It would sail from the port of Le Havre in two days' time.

I booked passage on it. Then I sent a telegraph to an old friend of mine. His name is John Lincoln. He teaches history in Montreal.

I arrived in Montreal two weeks later. John had done what I asked. He found me a cabin to rent. It was deep in the Canadian wilderness. I told him I wanted to be alone to finish writing a book.

I am in that cabin now. There is not another human being within two hundred miles.

I did not lie to John. I am finishing a book. This book.

It will be my final work as a scholar. It will be my ultimate contribution to knowledge of the werewolf.

Last night was the night of the full moon.

This morning I awoke lying on the floor. I felt wonderfully rested. It was as if a burden had been lifted from me. Or as if a terrible hunger had been satisfied.

I went exploring the nearby forest. I found a deer with its belly ripped open. And I found the remains of rabbits torn apart.

I now can state with certainty that it is true: He who is a werewolf remembers nothing of the horror.

There is nothing I can add to this. And only one thing left for me to do.

As for what I am writing, I am leaving it in an envelope. It is to be opened only by my cousin Sherlock. John Lincoln is coming to visit me

next week. I can trust him to send it to England.

When you read this, my dear Sherlock, do not mourn me.

Feel satisfaction that the mystery of the werewolf has been solved.

And pray that I can join in spirit with Marie. Pray that there is a place for us where the werewolf can never roam.

**Les Martin** has adapted many other Random House books for young readers, including *The Vampire*, *Oliver Twist*, *The Time Machine*, and *The Last of the Mohicans*. He also writes original action and adventure stories. An avid tennis player, he lives in New York City.

**Karen Chandler** loves drama and excitement. Her paintings of spaceship takeoffs and landings hang in the NASA space collection. *Edgar Allan Poe's Tales of Terror* was her first Random House book. She lives on Long Island.